ELI'S COMING

A SHORT STORY

By

T. M. Bilderback

Gretchen Cantrell looked around her best friend's "I got promoted" party, and felt let down. She tossed her shoulder-length blond hair behind her ears, and remembered what Cindy had said.

"Come to the party, Gretch! Please? Lots of good-looking, available guys will be there, I promise!" Cindy had begged the day before. "You'll find someone there to help you forget that dimwit you just dumped!"

"Cindy, please, will you just let me have a couple more days of my personal pity-party? I don't *want* anyone else right now. Burke sucked too much life out of me as it is!"

Cindy began to wring her hands, and then twist her auburn locks. "But,

Gretch-en, I don't want to have this party without you! *Pleeeeaaaassseee*?" Cindy had clasped her hands together, fingers entwined, and tucked them under her chin.

Gretchen, twenty-six years old to Cindy's twenty-five, rolled her eyes and said, "All *right*! If you will just stop whining!"

"Thankyou, thankyou, thankyou," Cindy began repeating, fast enough to make the two words sound as if they were only one, pulling Gretchen into a big bear hug while simultaneously jumping up and down. She pulled away, but left her hands on Gretchen's shoulders. "Oh, Gretch, I *promise* I'll make it up to you! I *promise*!"

Gretchen waved her friend off. "What-*ever*, Cindy! Jeez!"

Tonight, as she got off of the subway three blocks down from Cindy's loft apartment, Gretchen passed a sidewalk vendor that was seated at a folding table, with a draping velvet tablecloth over the top. He was seated directly in front of a coffee shop, with one chair across the table from him. He was dressed in a tan-colored robe, and had dark brown hair and dark brown eyes, so dark they were almost black. His hands were folded in front of him, almost in anticipation. Other people that passed him seemed as if they didn't see him. They avoided passing in front of him, and veered away from crossing the street at that spot. It was as if only she could see him.

As Gretchen approached, the man looked directly at her.

With an accent reminiscent of India or Pakistan, the vendor said, "May I tell your fortune?"

Gretchen stopped walking. She was debating what he said.

I'm really not in a hurry. I'm already late for the start of the party, and I didn't promise Cindy what time I'd get there. I also didn't promise what time I'd leave either. I'd get a kick out of getting my fortune read, but I'm not sure if I have the money.

As if he had read her mind, the vendor said, "I will be happy to tell you for only one dollar. Surely you have one dollar?" He reassured with his smile.

Gretchen returned the smile. "I have a dollar. Sure. Tell my future."

The vendor unfolded his hands and gestured to the opposite chair. "Please sit down."

Gretchen, still smiling, sat easily into the other chair. She noticed that now the other people passed by both of them, apparently without seeing either of them now.

The vendor held out his hand.

Gretchen looked at it, puzzled. She started to reach for it, but she realized that he was waiting for his dollar.

Smiling an embarrassed smile, Gretchen reached into her purse, and found a crumpled dollar bill. She passed it over to the vendor.

He bowed his head with grace, and said, "Thank you, Gretchen Cantrell." He tucked the dollar under his robe.

How did he know my name? Did I tell him my name? She looked at her open purse. Her mail was visible, with her name showing. *That's it! He saw it on my mail! Mystery solved.*

The vendor was looking at her intensely. "Eli's coming. You must hide your heart."

Gretchen shook her head slightly. "I…I don't understand. Who's coming?"

His voice had turned harsh and intense.

"That is all that I can tell you. You can walk, but you won't get away. Eli's coming, and you must hide your heart. I am not permitted to say more. Only that you must be aware that he is coming."

Gretchen abruptly stood up. "Now, look, mister...!"

She was alone on the sidewalk. The vendor was gone.

She looked all around her, but she didn't see a folding table, a velvet tablecloth, chairs...or the vendor.

And, for a brief, weird moment, no one else was on the sidewalk, as if everyone had vanished.

What the hell did I just see?

Gretchen shook her head as if to clear it.

I know he was here! He told me that Eli's coming!

A couple came out of the coffee shop and looked at Gretchen. She must have had a weird look on her face, because the couple kept looking at her warily as they walked away.

Great. Now I'm seeing things.

She continued toward Cindy's loft apartment with a drink on her mind.

***

So. Now that I'm here, now what? Gretchen almost felt that she had said that thought out loud. Then she looked around and realized that no one would have heard her if she had. The music was cranked up pretty loud in the loft apartment. *Out of the fifty people here, I know about three, and Cindy's so drunk that she hasn't even noticed I'm here.* Gretchen's friend was giggling madly in the center of a group of four men, looking much like a queen with her royal court of yes-men.

About half of the people were men, but no one seemed to interest Gretchen at all. The women were grouped together like herds of prey, using numbers to guard themselves against the predators gathered around them. The men were mostly just drinking, eating, laughing loudly at dirty jokes, and eyeing the women in their wary little groups. Occasionally, one of the men would peel off and attempt to have a conversation with one of the women, but none of them seemed to be able to get any of the women alone to attempt to talk to them. They wouldn't leave their groups.

Pity. And, tomorrow, all of the women will complain that the men here were lame, when there really are several that are quite attractive, if they'd just give them a chance. Gretchen threaded her way over to Cindy, and touched her arm.

Cindy turned with a smile on her face. The smile widened when she saw that it was Gretchen.

"*Gretch!*" said Cindy, with a loud voice. It had to be loud in order to be heard over the pounding of the music, and the laughter of the men. "You *made* it!" She grabbed Gretchen's arm and jumped with excitement.

Poor Cindy! Always so hyper!

Gretchen smiled back, and nodded. "I made it." She looked around.

"Seems like predators and prey at the watering hole at sunset."

Cindy looked puzzled, then laughed, even though she didn't understand the reference. "Yeah, it sure is! Everyone's having a *blast!* Let me introduce you to these guys! This is…" Cindy's voice droned on, and Gretchen only caught a couple of words. The rest she tuned out, because none of these guys held her interest.

Gretchen smiled and nodded and said, "Hi! How are you?" That was the extent of her conversations with Cindy's royal court. She turned to Cindy, and got close to her ear.

"I'm going to get a drink, Cin," Gretchen said, loud enough for Cindy to hear.

Cindy nodded. "Sure, Gretch! The bar's over there, and Stu is playing bartender!"

Stu. Wonderful. How many "exes" can ruin my "ohs"? Just one, like in Tic-Tac-Toe. Stu.

Gretchen headed in the direction that Cindy had pointed, and a makeshift bar had been set up against one wall. Stu Phillips was mixing drinks, heavy on the alcohol, and light on the soda.

It was actually a bit quieter at the bar. The decibels weren't as high as out in the middle of the room.

"Hi, Stu."

Stu looked up. When he saw Gretchen, his face lost all expression.

"Hello, Gretchen. How are you?"

"I've been better. How about you?"

Stu nodded. "I'm good. What kind of drink would you like? I still make a mean Mimosa."

She smiled and nodded. "That would be great, Stu."

"Coming up." Stu began mixing the drink. As he mixed, he stole occasional glances at Gretchen. "You know, Gretchen, I'm glad we ran into each other…"

"Don't, Stu." Gretchen was abrupt. "Not now."

Stu's face lost expression again. "I was only going to apologize to you for some of the things I said when we broke up."

Gretchen looked at the man. She sighed. "I'm sorry, Stu. I shouldn't have snapped at you. I just had another rough breakup, and I thought you were going to hit on me, and say we should try again."

Stu smiled a thin smile. "Not a chance, Gretchen. Our split was mutual. I don't want to be back with you any more than you want to be back with me." He handed the Mimosa to her. "We said some pretty mean things to each other there at the end, and I wanted to apologize for some of the things I said."

Gretchen smiled a tiny smile. "Some?"

Stu returned the smile, and nodded. "Yes. Some. And I'll let you forever wonder about which ones I'm sorry about. Enjoy your drink."

"Thanks. Jerk." She turned away and faced the crowd.

And saw him.

He was across the room, leaning against the wall. His legs were crossed at the ankles as he stood, with on foot on pointe. His brown hair was longish, but it was not quite shoulder length. He wore jeans, boots, and a blue plaid flannel shirt, with the sleeves rolled midway up his forearm. His lips were full, but not too full. They were just the type of lips that promised to deliver a great kiss, whether it was a passionate soul kiss, or a gentle brush of those lips on a woman's cheek. Gretchen could see his eyes, even from this distance, were a bright blue, and as penetrating as a strong winter breeze from the north.

He was looking at Gretchen, too, and she found herself melting inside. She felt desire tingling, along with a silent desire to make passionate love to this man.

But, first, she had to find out his name.

Gretchen weaved her way through the room. Her eyes never left his as she walked. It seemed as if she walked in slow motion, but it also seemed like she moved at the speed of light. His eyes held her, drew her to him, and melted her soul.

"Hi," she said, once she got to his side.

"Hi." He smiled gently at her.

Gretchen felt herself melt inside when she heard his voice. *Why can't I take my eyes away from him?*

"I'm Gretchen Cantrell."

He nodded knowingly. "Gretchen Cantrell. Nice name."

Hearing his voice as he spoke her name made her knees weak, but she continued to stand.

Stammering a bit, Gretchen said, "S-so. What's your name?"

He smiled a small smile, and looked deeply into her eyes. "Does it matter?"

Almost as if she were hypnotized, Gretchen slowly shook her head.

He stood upright, and turned toward her. He was only three inches taller than her, although she didn't register the fact. That made him about five-ten. He was facing her fully now, and it felt as if he were looking directly into her soul with those bright blue eyes.

"Gretchen. Do you want me?"

Slowly, she nodded. "Oh, yes. I want you."

He nodded toward the loft door with his head. "Then let's go."

Gretchen left the party without a goodbye, and with a man she'd never met, and whose name she didn't know.

***

Gretchen took the man back to her apartment, a one-bedroom walkup in midtown.

She closed the door behind them, put her purse on the table beside the door, and turned to him. When she spoke, her voice trembled.

"Excuse the mess here."

He looked around the room. "What mess?"

Gretchen waved her hand around the room. "In here." She put her hand at her side, and then raised it again to tap her chest with one finger. "And in here."

He smiled, and looked into her eyes. "One of those can be fixed quickly. The other can be taken care of, with time and…well…some sort of action, I guess."

She still hadn't looked into his eyes since they had arrived at her apartment.

"Would…would you like something to drink?" asked Gretchen.

He considered. "A glass of juice would be wonderful."

She toyed with her necklace. "Is orange okay?"

"That's fine."

Gretchen went to the kitchen, got a glass, and got the juice from the refrigerator. As she poured, she berated herself.

What are you doing? You don't even know this guy's name! What are you expecting, a night of wild passion?

She picked up the glass and turned to return to the living room, but he was right there, behind her. Startled, she dropped the glass, which broke all over the floor. She made some kind of noise, and looked into those cool blue eyes.

But, they weren't blue anymore.

They were red, glowing...and growing larger.

Gretchen found that she couldn't move. His eyes held her in place.

And she was terrified.

"Some things are better left unsaid, don't you think?"

She tried to nod at his remark, but couldn't move her head.

"Things like heartache...burning heartache. One shouldn't talk about it. It might draw...*unsavory* attention."

Gretchen discovered that she was lost in those red eyes. Nothing else mattered. Except...

"My name?" he said, reaching to touch the center of her chest. His hand passed through her skin, into her body. It caused a dull ache, sort of the way a healing cut feels if you accidentally hit it against something.

She could feel his fingers closing tightly around her heart.

"I have been called Eli." His head jerked backward, as he derived both pleasure and sustenance from her heartache. Involuntarily, his hand squeezed tightly.

Gretchen's head also jerked backward, as the energy of her heart left her body, passing through the tendrils of energy that were Eli's fingers, and into Eli's corporeal form.

Gretchen's heart burst, her eyes widened in death, and she collapsed onto the floor, and into the orange juice that lay puddled there.

Eli's hand slipped out of her chest as she fell and left no trace of its passing. The skin on her chest appeared untouched.

"You can never get away from the burning heartache, Gretchen."

***

Three days later, Cindy was learning her new job. She really enjoyed it, and was amazed at the respect she received from other employees. Advertising was great when everyone listened to *your* ideas.

She had just gotten back to her desk after a client meeting, when her desk phone rang.

"Hi, this is Cindy Frazier. How may I help you?"

"Hi, Cindy, this is Stu."

"Hey, Stu! Listen, I'm kinda busy right now. What's up?"

"Have you heard from Gretchen lately?"

"No, now that you mention it, I haven't heard from her since the party."

"Apparently, no one has."

"What do you mean?"

"I tried to call her to apologize for an argument at your party, and I got no answer. I tried calling her at work, but they said she hasn't been in for a few days, and that she hasn't called, either.

They're getting ready to fire her if she doesn't show up tomorrow. Cindy, I'm worried about her."

"Wow. That isn't like her."

"I know. What can we do?"

"Hmm...let me try to call her. Maybe she's just taking calls from you. I'll call you back right after I try, okay?"

"Sounds good, Cindy. Thanks."

Cindy disconnected the phone, and dialed her friend's cell. After several rings, it went to voicemail. Cindy disconnected the call, and called Stu.

"She didn't answer me, either."

"Listen, I'm off work in an hour. Why don't I come by your building and pick you up? We can swing over to her apartment and check on her. I still have a key."

"You didn't give it back when you guys split?"

Stu chuckled. "She never gave me the chance."

Cindy laughed. "That's her, all right. Sounds like a plan. See you soon."

"I'll be there. Bye, Cindy."

"Bye."

That's weird. Gretchen wouldn't just skip work without telling them something.

As she began putting together the ad package that her client had approved, Cindy racked her brain for any hints that Gretchen might have given.

Did I miss something? I barely said hello to her at the party, and I've been busy

the last few days, so I haven't called her. I
don't even remember her leaving the party.
Was I that drunk?

Gretch is probably just shacked up,
enjoying her pity party. She'll answer the
door, and call us a couple of assholes for
worrying.

I hope.

***

Stu knocked on Gretchen's
apartment door.

"Damn, Stu! Wake the dead, why
don't you?" Cindy was looking around
to see if anyone was looking at them,
but the hallway was empty.

"Just want to make sure that she
can hear it, Cin."

"Gyahh! I think the whole building heard it!" She pressed her ear against Gretchen's door. "I don't hear anything." She stood up straight again. "Knock again."

This time, Stu pounded on the door.

There still was no sound from inside.

Stu took out his wallet, took the door key from it, and inserted it into the lock. He unlocked the door, and they were greeted by a faint odor.

"Oh, my God," said Cindy quietly.

Stu pushed the door open. "Cindy, get your cell out, and be ready to call nine-one-one. But I think it may be too late."

They slowly entered the apartment. The blinds were closed, and no lights were on. Cindy reached for the light switch, and turned it on.

There was nothing in the living room.

Both of them were holding their hands over their noses now, and breathing through their mouths.

"Bedroom?" asked Cindy.

Stu nodded.

They opened the bedroom door. Nothing. And nothing in the bathroom.

Stu braced himself. "The only thing left is the kitchen."

Cindy nodded.

Gretchen was still on the floor. Her body seemed very pale, and her stomach seemed distended. The orange juice had since turned into a pale, sticky mess, and Gretchen's face still held the look of surprise she had when she had died.

Stu and Cindy ran from the apartment, and closed the door behind them.

Cindy collapsed into Stu's arms.

"Oh, Stu, she'd dead!"

"I know, Cindy."

Cindy was crying. Stu took her phone and called the police.

"My name is Stuart Mitchell. I need an ambulance at…"

***

The coroner ruled that Gretchen's death was a heart attack, and the time of death was sometime between ten PM and midnight on the night of Cindy's party.

Stu had found out this information from the police detective that had initially questioned him after he had called in Gretchen's death. It was treated as a homicide until the coroner's ruling, and the detective was one of the few that actually let a possible "person of interest" know when the police were no longer interested in them.

Stu called Cindy so that he could tell her about the coroner' ruling.

"Stu, that's just crazy! Gretchen never had a problem with her heart! Not once in her entire life. She would have said something to me."

Stu was nodding as his Blue Tooth device shone blue light from his left ear. "I know, Cindy, but that's what the coroner said." He stopped at the corner to cross the street, on his way to lunch. "As close as we were for a time, she would have told me, too, if there had been anything to tell."

"Wow. Listen, Stu, I have a meeting with my boss and a client. Big advertising campaign coming up. Can we meet for dinner, and talk about it then?"

Stu smiled, in spite of himself. "Sure. Where?"

"How about that new place? You know, Apollo…it's down by the bay."

"Sounds good. Want to meet in the Bay Park at seven?"

"You read my mind, Stuart. I'll see you there!"

Stu tapped his earpiece to disconnect the call.

***

Stu sat on a wood and wrought iron bench in Bay Park as he waited for Cindy. It was on the dark side of dusk, and the lights along the park path were just beginning to light up. He looked around the park, and he seemed to be alone, for the moment.

Stu looked at his phone to check the time, and saw that it was five minutes past seven. Cindy should be along any time now.

He looked up again. On Stu's right, between his park bench and the Apollo Restaurant, about twenty feet away, a street vendor had set up a table.

That was fast. He wasn't there a minute ago! Where did he come from?

The table had a dark velvet covering draped over it. Two metal folding chairs were across the table from the vendor. The man seated at the table wore a tan-colored, almost khaki robe. His hair was dark, and he had an olive-colored complexion. His hands were folded together, and the man seemed to have a calm demeanor.

Why here? And what's he selling? Whatever it is, he's not going to make a lot of money here. There's no one in the park but me!

"Hey, Stu!" said Cindy.

Stu jumped, and said, "Oh, crap! You really scared me, Cindy!"

Cindy laughed, and pointed back down the sidewalk on Stu's left. "I came in through the west entrance. Sorry I scared you! I'm surprised you didn't hear my heels clacking!"

Stu stood, and shook his head with an embarrassed shake.

"Sorry. I was lost in thought, and just didn't hear you." He crooked his left arm at the elbow, inviting her to take his arm. "Ready to eat?"

Cindy hooked her arm into Stu's. "Oh, God, yes! I'm starving!"

The two friends began walking. As they passed the man sitting at the folding table, the man spoke to them.

"May I tell your fortunes?"

Stu and Cindy stopped for a moment, and looked at the seated man.

Stu shook his head slightly, and said, "I don't think so, friend. Thanks anyway."

They turned to leave the man, but he spoke again, freezing them in their tracks.

"Your friend, Gretchen, allowed me to tell her fortune. Although she did not heed the advice that I gave, I did give her advice, and I did give her fortune. I offer it to you as well, if you're willing to listen."

Slowly, and with much hesitation, the two friends turned back to the man.

Stu, indignant, said, "Just what do you know about Gretchen, buddy?"

Patting Stu on the chest, Cindy said, "Maybe we should call the police, Stu."

The seated man smiled. "The police will not help you, and I would be gone before they arrived." He gestured to the two chairs across from him. "Will you please sit down? I will tell you what I can."

Stu stared at the man, then looked into Cindy's eyes. Cindy nodded slightly. They sat down.

"I regret that I must ask each of you for one dollar. It's the rule that I must follow." The man held out his hand, palm up.

Stu actually thought about spitting into the man's hand, but, instead, dug out a dollar bill from his wallet and gave it to the man. Cindy had scrounged around in her purse and found four quarters, which she also placed into the man's hand.

"Thank you." The man tucked the money inside his robe, and folded his hands in front of him again.

"What're our fortunes?" asked Stu.

The man looked from Stu to Cindy, and then spoke.

"Eli's coming. You must hide your hearts."

Stu and Cindy waited for the man to continue, but he was silent.

"That's it?" asked Stu. He felt anger growing inside.

"It is all I am allowed to tell you."

Cindy asked, "Who is Eli?"

"Eli is a demon. He disguises himself as a very attractive human, but he is a demon."

"And you told this to Gretchen?" spat Stu.

"I told her that Eli was coming, and that she had to hide her heart. I did not have opportunity to tell her more. She stood after I told her that, and did not ask questions. Once a customer stands, the transaction is complete. I could tell her no more."

Cindy looked puzzled. "So, if we sit here, you'll explain everything we need to know?"

"As much as I can. Of course, you must ask the proper questions."

Stu was incredulous. He turned to Cindy. "You're not really believing this, are you?"

Cindy put a hand on Stu's arm to calm him. "Let's hear him out, Stu. What could it hurt?"

Stu shook his head, then took a deep breath and muttered, "Okay, Cindy."

Cindy turned to the fortune teller. "You say Eli is a demon?"

"Yes."

"Did he kill Gretchen?"

"Yes."

"How?"

"Eli feeds on heartache. It is his sustenance. Gretchen's heartache called to him, and he could not refuse the invitation to partake."

Cindy thought for a moment, then turned to Stu. "Gretchen left the party with some guy that I'd never seen before. Did you see them?"

Stu thought about it. "I saw her talking to some guy against the wall." He shrugged. "I didn't pay much attention after that. The wound is still a little raw, you know?"

"Eli's coming. Hide your heart, Stu." The fortune teller looked at Stu with concern. "Eli can take any form that is attractive to his prey. You must be cautious."

Stu wrinkled his brow. "Why are you telling us? Is this 'Eli' coming for us?"

"Yes, Stu. He sensed heartache from both of you at your party, Cindy.

Gretchen's heartache was stronger, so he chose her. But he will return for both of you. His hunger is never sated for long."

"So, he can be either a man or a woman?" asked Stu.

"Eli can be any form that is attractive to you. Man, woman, child, animal, or plant. Eli could be anything." The man spread his hands. "I use the pronoun 'him' or 'he', but Eli is neither...and both."

"Can Eli be killed?" asked Cindy.

The man shook his head. "No."

"Can he be stopped?" Cindy replied.

"Yes."

"How?"

The man smiled, as if approving her question. "I have a vessel." He put his hand inside his robe. When he drew it back out, it held an ancient-looking vase, with a long, thin neck, and a bulbous bottom. It had a large wooden plug in the top. "Eli can be trapped inside this. He remains until he is again released to prey once more." He held the vase out to Stu.

Stu just had one thought running through his mind: *How did this guy have that big vase hidden inside his robe? He's so skinny! There's no room for anything else inside that robe!* He reached out and took the vase. He pulled out the plug and asked, "Okay. How does it work?"

The man smiled, and again reached into his robe. He pulled out two three by five index cards, and handed one to Stu, and then to Cindy.

"You will repeat the words written on these cards. Once the demon is inside the bottle, you will put the plug back in. I will take the bottle from you, and take care of putting the bottle away so that there isn't any more trouble with Eli."

Both friends looked at the index cards.

Cindy said, "Does pronunciation count?"

The vendor smiled. "No."

Stu asked, "Does it have to be this language? Won't an English translation work?"

The man shook his head as he smiled. "No, it must be in this ancient language. I did spell the words phonetically, however. You should have no trouble pronouncing them."

Cindy started to read her card out loud.

"No! You must not say the words until it is time to put the demon into the vessel! If you say them now, it will only summon him here!"

Stu looked at the vendor. "Will you help us? Let us know when he shows up?"

The vendor shook his head slowly. "No. I can do no more than I am doing now."

Cindy's eyes brightened. "You said that saying these words now would summon the demon. Why couldn't we summon him here and repeat the words once he arrives?"

The vendor smiled. "You can, but it must not be here. It must be elsewhere, with many other people surrounding you, for your own protection."

"Why?" asked Stu. "He can't do anything once the words are spoken, can he?"

The vendor's face turned grim. "No, but the demon can take you into the bottle as well, if you are within reach. I urge you to be cautious."

Cindy thought for a moment. "Is there anything else that I need to know that I'm haven't asked?"

The vendor smiled. "Yes."

Cindy smiled back. "But you can't tell me unless I specifically ask, right?"

"Correct."

"How about my love life?"

The vendor answered, but showed no expression. "Assuming that you can defeat the demon, your future, in that respect, lies with one you already know."

Cindy's thoughts ran through her head quickly, and she stole a quick glance at Stu. She then looked immediately at the vendor's eyes.

She could see the smile hiding in them.

She had her answer.

Cindy Frasier stood up.

Stu fell to the ground when the chair he was sitting in disappeared, along with the vendor.

***

Seated at their booth inside Apollo, the waiter took their drink orders, and said that he'd be back to take their orders in a few minutes.

Both of them were looking at their menus, but Cindy kept stealing glances at Stu over the top.

Finally, Cindy couldn't stand the silence.

"What looks good to you, Stu?"

"The steak and lobster plate looks really good to me. What looks good to you, Cindy?"

Cindy met his eyes above the menu.

I'm really tempted to say, 'you', but I'm not going to. Not yet. Not until we get

rid of this demon, and not until I know how
he feels about me.

"I think I'm leaning toward a salad. Bleu Cheese dressing."

The waiter arrived right on time, and took their orders.

"Do you still have the cards with the words, Cindy?"

"Of course."

"May I see them?"

Cindy took the cards out of her purse, and passed them across the table to Stu.

Stu looked them over. Then, he looked at her as he put the index cards beside his plate.

"We should do it now."

Cindy said, "Huh?"

"We should do it now. We're in a crowded restaurant, surrounded by people. We should summon the demon now, and put him away."

Cindy looked around at the diners in the restaurant. She turned back to Stu.

"Do you really think we should?"

"Why not?"

"Do you think it would be dangerous?"

"I'm not convinced of any of it, Cindy. If the demon shows, we can repeat the words, and put the demon in the jar that the vendor gave us."

The waiter arrived, carrying their drinks on a tray. Once he left, Cindy pulled the bottle-shaped jar from her purse.

"Here it is. Who says the words, and who holds the jar?"

Stu's brow furrowed.

"I...I hadn't really thought about, Cin. I'm not really sure that I completely believe it, anyway."

"Well, you had better make up your mind fast, Stuart! I need your help with this! I can't do it alone!" Cindy was whispering with urgency.

Stu put up his hands, palms toward Cindy. "Okay, okay! I believe, for Gretchen's sake!"

As Cindy opened her mouth to say something else, a beautifully shaped hand, with long, painted fingernails, touched Stu on the shoulder.

Both Cindy and Stu turned to look at the owner of the hand.

It was a woman. Her eyes were large and blue, and she had black hair that draped to the middle of her back. Her hair had a healthy sheen. Her skin was as white as porcelain. She stood about five-two, and was extremely attractive.

Stu was mesmerized. He couldn't take his eyes off of her.

Cindy, however, was mistrustful of the woman on sight.

"Pardon me for intruding," the woman said to Stu. Her voice was low and sultry. "But I find you *very* attractive. Would you like to get out of here?"

The woman ran her finger under Stu's chin.

Stu nodded as if he were hypnotized. He stood up slowly, and the couple began walking away from the table.

Cindy was thunderstruck. She had seen it, but she didn't believe it. *He's being led away like a puppy on a leash!*

Suddenly a small folding table appeared in the middle of the restaurant. It was covered with a dark velvet covering. Cindy realized that it was the vendor's table.

If it's the vendor's table, he must be telling me something...like that woman is the demon!

The table disappeared.

Cindy picked up the index cards, pulled the plug from the top of the bottle, and began reciting the words printed there.

"*Nocte delibium candas cor de…*"

The woman whirled around so quickly that Stu was knocked into a booth with four diners. Food, drinks, and tableware scattered loudly.

The woman's eyes were no longer blue. They were red, and her face began elongating. Her hands grew into long, claw-like fingers, and she ran toward Cindy.

Cindy saw her coming, and realized that the demon would be on her before she finished the incantation…unless something intervened, and intervened quickly.

Unfortunately, nothing happened to stop the demon. It had changed so much that it no longer resembled a woman…or a man. It was something in-between, with fierce, red eyes and a long, lupine face. It hit Cindy hard, and knocked her to the floor.

People through the restaurant were screaming. Many were running out the exits.

The demon held both of Cindy's wrists pinned above her head, wrapped easily in one hand. The other hand was free, and the demon stared into Cindy's eyes. It spoke to her, and its voice was deep and gutteral.

"So you know what I am. I don't know where you found that incantation, but you'll never finish it."

It closed its eyes, and its nostrils flared. It seemed to be searching for a scent.

"Ahhhh-hh-h-h," it said. "I feel your heartache! I sense the burning of your heart!"

Its nostrils flared once again as it inhaled.

"Yessss…not as deep as the pig Gretchen, and not as powerful as the man, but tasty enough…and enough to whet my appetite!"

It placed its hand on Cindy's chest.

***

Stu shook his head to clear it. As he became aware of his surroundings once again, he noticed that he was in the middle of a table…but no one was in the booth. He had time to wonder how he had gotten there, and then he heard the demon.

Stu jumped from the table and saw Cindy pinned under the demon. A quick glance told him what had happened. Cindy had saved him by reciting the words, but, for some reason, had not finished. Now, unless he hurried, Cindy was done for.

Stu realized that, more than anything, he wanted Cindy to live…and to be a part of his life. Subconsciously, he thought that he might have wanted that ever since Gretchen had introduced them.

But, now, he needed to distract the demon.

As Stu scanned the restaurant, he saw that many of the patrons had left. There was chaos and noise. Stu saw one of the chefs standing in the kitchen door. Stu pointed at the man.

"*You!* Meat cleaver! *Now!*"

A look of surprise crossed the face of the mustachioed man in the tall chef's hat, and then realization. The man reached inside the kitchen. When his hand again appeared, he held one of the biggest meat cleavers that Stu had ever seen. The chef threw the cleaver toward Stu.

Stu reached up and plucked the cleaver out of the air, smoothly grabbing the handle as the cleaver twirled to him. Later, he would be amazed that he had done this, but, now, his mind was only on one thing: saving Cindy.

Stu ran to the demon just as it put its hand on Cindy's chest.

It's now or never!

Stu raised the cleaver and brought it down with all his strength. The cleaver struck the back of the demon's neck, and almost severed its head. The demon whirled, and again tried to hit Stu…but Stu was no longer there. He had danced around to the demon's side. When the demon whirled, Stu struck again with the cleaver, once more using all of his strength.

The demon's head left the body, and rolled under a table.

Screams came from the patrons still inside the restaurant.

Stu looked around, wondering why they were screaming. He had removed the demon's head…surely there was nothing else to scream about.

"Stu!"

Cindy had gotten out from under the demon, and did a backwards crabwalk away from it.

The demon wasn't dead.

It had released Cindy's wrists because its body was feeling around the floor for its head. Luckily, when its head rolled under the table after being removed from its body, the demon's eyes were facing away from its body, and it couldn't direct its searching hands without being able to see.

Cindy picked up the index cards again and began reciting the words once more.

The jar was still on the table that Stu and Cindy had occupied until a few minutes ago.

"…*hydryat cor daemonde!*" finished Cindy.

The demon found its head just as Cindy finished the incantation. Its head screamed loudly and painfully. It began stretching and whirling as if it was caught in a tornado. Wind whipped all through the restaurant, and the noise was deafening. The demon then disappeared into the jar. When it did, Stu was there, and slammed the plug into the top.

The wind died away, and the remaining patrons looked around the restaurant with caution.

Stu went to Cindy, and swept her into his arms.

"Oh, man, did we just do that?" he said into her hair.

Cindy slowly wrapped her arms around Stu, and gradually tightened.

"Yeah, I think we did, Stu."

"You did indeed accomplish the task. I will take the jar from you now, and dispose of it properly."

The voice came from beside them. It was the vendor. He was smiling broadly.

Stu and Cindy both laughed. They were relieved and proud of what they had accomplished.

Stu turned to the table and picked up the jar. He held it out to the vendor, who took it and put it away inside his robe.

The vendor bowed with his head.

"I thank you both. I will now make certain that there will be no…repercussions…for you."

The vendor waved his arms and disappeared.

The restaurant had been returned to its original condition. Not a plate was broken, not a chair was out of place anywhere in the restaurant. The people were back, and many of them were staring at Cindy and Stu, because the couple were standing in the middle of the dining floor.

They realized where they were, and were a little disoriented by the sudden change. Stu waved slightly, and both were grinning sheepish grins as they went back to their booth.

Once seated, Cindy leaned over to Stu and whispered.

"Are we the only ones that remember what happened?"

Stu looked around. Finally, he nodded.

"I think so."

Their food was there, but neither of them ate much. After they had pushed their food around on the plate, Stu had had enough.

"Cindy, let's get out of here, okay?"

Cindy put down her fork.

"Sounds great!"

Stu paid the check.

As the couple walked through the park, Stu timidly reached for Cindy's hand.

Cindy took it, and squeezed.

Both of the young people smiled in the moonlight.

After a couple of minutes, they came to a small, folding table, covered with a dark velvet cloth. A single envelope was on it.

They exchanged glances, and Cindy picked up the envelope. Inside was an index card.

They both knew who the card was from.

It read simply, *Heartache and deep feelings make us who we are. Cherish each other.*

Stu looked into Cindy's eyes. Both of them saw what they needed to see.

And they didn't need a fortune teller to explain it to them.

###

About The Author: T. M. Bilderback is a former radio announcer with a number of story ideas running around inside his head, most based on or inspired by classic songs. The author currently resides in Tennessee, and is writing feverishly in order to banish these stories from his head and into book form before he runs screaming into the street.

Other works by T. M. Bilderback

Nicholas Turner
If You Could Read My Mind

Justice Security
Mama Told Me Not To Come
Someone Saved My Life Tonight
Jackie Blue
Wake Me Up Before You Go-Go
Saturday In The Park
MacArthur Park
The Little Drummer Boy
The Night Chicago Died
Jim Dandy
Cow Patty
Hell's Bells

Tales Of Sardis County
Don't Come Around Here No More
Junior's Farm
The Devil's In The Details
I'm Your Boogie Man

Colonel Abernathy's Tales
The Lion Sleeps Tonight
Heart Of Glass

Other Stories
The Wreck Of The Edmund Fitzgerald
Gold
Hot Child In The City
Eli's Coming

Other Novels
Empty Eyes

Story Collections
Greatest Hits

www.ingramcontent.com/pod-product-compliance
Lightning Source LLC
Chambersburg PA
CBHW022051170626
46808CB00003B/1437